ISBN 0 86112 436 7
© BRIMAX BOOKS LTD 1987. All rights reserved.
Published by Brimax Books, Newmarket, England 1987.
The stories in this book previously appeared in
a smaller format as Animal Bedtime Stories.
Printed in Belgium.

NIGHT-TIME TALES

Illustrated by Eric Kincaid

Stories by Lucy Kincaid

CONTENTS

A Wet Night   8

Lost and Found   15

A Problem   21

Was It Real?   28

Something Prickly   35

The Secret   41

A . . A . . Something   48

A Night Out   55

BRIMAX · NEWMARKET · ENGLAND

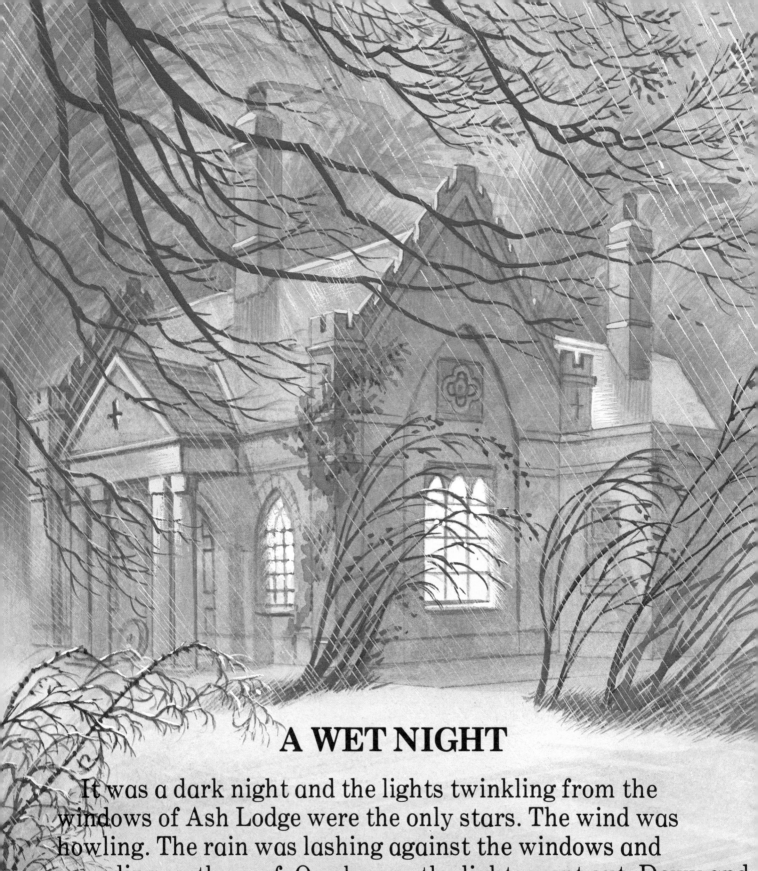

A WET NIGHT

It was a dark night and the lights twinkling from the windows of Ash Lodge were the only stars. The wind was howling. The rain was lashing against the windows and pounding on the roof. One by one the lights went out. Dewy and Basil the two badgers, and Willie the mole, had gone to bed.

Willie tried to shut out the noise of the wind. He put his paws over his ears. That didn't work. He put on his woolly hat. That didn't work either. He was trying to think what to do next when he felt something plop on to his face. Rain was coming in . . . through the ceiling.

9

"DEWY!" he called loudly, as he tumbled out of bed and switched on the light. "DEWY! BASIL! COME QUICKLY!"

He was standing on his bed trying to catch the drips in a paper cup when Basil appeared in the doorway.

"What is it?" asked Basil with a wide yawn.

"Can't you see! It's dripping!" said Willie crossly. "Do something . . . I can't stand here like this all night."

"I say . . ." said Dewy looking over Basil's shoulder. "There's water coming through the ceiling."

"Help me push Willie's bed against the wall before it gets wet," said Basil. And without waiting for Willie to get down, or even sit down, he and Dewy pushed.

"OOOPS! Sorry!" said Basil. Willie had fallen over backwards and was bouncing up and down as though he was on a trampoline. The drips he had collected so carefully splashed over his face and gave him a sudden cold water wash.

"You might warn me when you're going to do something like that," he spluttered.

"It was an emergency . . . had to act quickly," said Dewy.

"Wind must have blown a slate off the roof," said Basil. "We'll go up and take a look in the morning."

"Why can't you go now?" asked Willie sliding quickly into bed and pulling the blankets round his chin.

"Well, for one thing it's dark," said Basil. "And for another it's raining, and . . ."

"You'll be sorry if you come to wake me in the morning and find I've floated away," said Willie.

"There won't be a flood," laughed Dewy as he put a bucket to catch the drips.

PING . . . PING . . . PING . . . PING . . . PING . . .

"I can't possibly sleep with THAT noise going on," grumbled Willie. But he did.

When he woke it was morning and the sun was shining. It had stopped raining some time during the night, for the bucket was only half full. There was barely enough water in it to make a puddle. Dewy and Basil were outside looking up at the roof.

"I was right," said Basil. "There IS a slate off. We'll get up there and mend it right away."

"What about my breakfast?" asked Willie.

"That will have to wait," said Basil. "Someone must hold the ladder."

Willie got bored holding the ladder and went up onto the roof to see what Basil and Dewy were doing.

"What are YOU doing up HERE?" demanded Basil.
"LOOK OUT!" shouted Dewy. "THE LADDER'S SLIPPING!"
The ladder fell to the ground with a THUD, and there
they all were, on the roof, with no way of getting down.
It was much too far to jump.

"It's all Willie's fault," said Dewy crossly.

"I don't know why you're fussing," said Willie brightly. "I'll put it back." And before Dewy or Basil could stop him he had tucked his legs round the drainpipe and was sliding towards the ground . . . and the water barrel.

"Oh dear," said Basil quietly as Willie went into the barrel like a cork, and water came out like a fountain.

"Are you alright?" called Dewy anxiously.

"Of course I'm not," spluttered Willie. "I'm WET . . ." He caught hold of the drainpipe and pulled himself out. It wasn't easy. The water ran from his fur in streams and made a pool round his feet. He began to squeeze his fur dry.

"Put the ladder back before you do that," called Basil.

"I might catch cold," said Willie. He made them wait until he had squeezed out the very last drip. THEN he put the ladder back. THEN he remembered he hadn't had breakfast so he stood on the bottom rung and held it steady while Basil and Dewy came down. If he made them TOO cross they might make him get breakfast and that wouldn't suit him at all.

LOST AND FOUND

Dewy was re-arranging the store cupboard. Willie was helping.

"Hand me that bag of flour next," said Dewy.

"Look out!" shouted Basil from the other side of the room. "The bo . . ." But he was too late. As Willie handed the bag across to Dewy, the bottom came undone and flour poured onto the rug like a cascading waterfall.

"Atishoo!" sneezed Willie as he was lost in the middle of a white cloud.

"Atishoo!" sneezed Dewy. HE looked like a snowbadger.

"Oh dear," said Basil. "What a mess!"

When the cloud of flour settled there was a layer of white dust everywhere. Basil took charge. Dewy and Willie were sneezing too much to be able to think properly.

"Willie, you take the rug outside and get it clean," he said. "Dewy and I will clean up in here."

Willie pulled the rug out onto the grass and began to whack it with the carpet beater.

Whack! "ATISHOO!" Whack! "ATISHOO!" The harder Willie whacked the bigger the cloud got. It was half an hour before the colours on the rug showed through again.

"The rug is whacked and so am I," he sighed as he left it on the grass and went indoors to get a drink.

"Willie!" Basil was calling from the garden.
"What is it?" asked Willie, alarmed by Basil's frown.
"You didn't have to beat the rug THAT hard," said Basil accusingly. Willie gasped. There was a large bare patch right in its middle.

17

"How did that get there?" he asked.

"That's what I want to know," said Basil crossly.

"I didn't do it," said Willie. "It was alright when I left it . . . really it was." And he looked so innocent Basil had to believe him.

"Holes like that don't come by themselves," said Dewy. "I want to know where all the pieces of wool have gone."

"Perhaps the wind blew them away," said Willie.

Dewy tested for wind. "There isn't any," he said.

There wasn't a scrap of coloured wool anywhere on the grass . . . or on any of the bushes . . . or anywhere else.

"Very odd," said Basil, scratching his head. "Very odd indeed. I don't understand this at all."

There was a polite cough behind them.

"Er . . . does this belong to you?" asked a voice. They turned and saw a very embarrassed-looking dormouse. She was struggling with a large bundle of loose woollen pieces.

"They're from OUR rug," said Willie indignantly. "What are YOU doing with them?"

"I think you'd better explain," said Basil sternly.

The dormouse sighed. "It's getting close to the time when we dormice settle down for our winter sleep," she said. "The children were only trying to help. When they saw the rug they thought how snug it would keep us through the winter, so they helped themselves to a little piece of it."

"A little piece . . ." sniffed Willie. "That doesn't look like a little piece to me."

"There's some more of it at home," sighed the dormouse. "I couldn't carry it all. You had better come and get it."

But when they arrived at the dormouse home they found the dormice children already curled up and asleep in a rainbow-coloured bed.

"They didn't waste any time, did they?" said Willie.

They looked so cosy and warm Dewy would not let their mother wake them.

"Let them sleep on," he said.
"But what about your rug?" said the dormouse.
"We'll find something to mend it with," said Basil.
"Don't you worry any more." And that is why one of the rugs
in Ash Lodge has a brown middle and rainbow-coloured borders.

20

A PROBLEM

The Ash Lodge pond stretches between the trees as though it is part of a winding river. It is possible to walk all round it of course, but more and more often, the badgers and Willie found themselves ferrying their friends across the middle of it, on their raft.

If someone had an errand to do on the far side of the pond, they would call in at Ash Lodge, and drop hints about how much time it would save if only they could go across the pond, instead of round it.

"This is such a useful shortcut," said Hannah Hedgehog as Basil ferried her across one morning.

"I can see that it must be," said Basil, trying not to sigh as Hannah settled herself comfortably. He had been sitting comfortably himself, making plans for the day, when Hannah had called.

"You've no idea how long it used to take me to walk all the way round the edge of the pond," she said brightly. "I've got rather short legs you know. I was always arriving too late for EVERYTHING."

"You won't forget to keep a look out and come across for me when I return, will you?" she said as she stepped ashore.

There were three dormice lazing on the bank.

"Knew you'd come, sooner or later," they said, "didn't feel like walking." They scrambled onto the raft without so much as a by-your-leave and lay on their backs with their tails trailing in the water while Basil did all the work.

"Thanks for the lift, Baz!" they called cheekily as they hopped off on the opposite bank.

"Oh dear," sighed Basil when he got back to the house. "I feel tired already and the day has hardly begun. Perhaps we should sink the raft and put a stop to all this ferrying backwards and forwards."

"We couldn't possibly do that!" exclaimed Dewy. "Our friends rely on us."

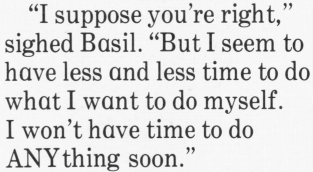

"I suppose you're right," sighed Basil. "But I seem to have less and less time to do what I want to do myself. I won't have time to do ANYthing soon."

"You're exaggerating," laughed Dewy. But when he had to put his book down in the middle of an exciting chapter to go across the pond and bring Hannah back, HE sighed too, and said, "I wish there was another way of crossing the pond."

"Pity there isn't a bridge," said Willie.

"Willie, you're a genius!" cried Basil. "We'll build a bridge."

"Who? US?" asked Willie disbelievingly.

"Do you think we could?" asked Dewy.

"I don't see why not," said Basil.

They asked Otley Otter to help them. He was used to working under water. As they rolled the logs into the pond he roped them together. When there were enough to stretch right across the pond he anchored them firmly, so that they would not float away. They all agreed they could never have made the bridge without his help.

"How would YOU like to be the first to use the new bridge?" Basil asked Otley.

"Well," said Otley, "as you know, I usually swim across the pond, but just this once I think I WILL walk."

"I announce this bridge officially open," he said as everyone followed him across.

Otley promised to keep a special watch on the underneath side of the bridge to see that none of the logs broke loose and he also promised to rescue anyone who was foolish enough to fall off the bridge and into the pond.

"I'll be special bridge-keeper and life guard," he laughed.

For the next few days the bridge was as busy as a town street. Everyone found a good reason for going across at least twice a day and if they hadn't a real reason they made one up. Willie was the one who fell off it, of course. Basil said he would have been MORE surprised if Willie hadn't fallen off. The splash he made as he fell in sent the water bouncing in waves against the banks. It made the logs rock dizzily and frightened all the ducks. Otley managed to catch hold of him before he swallowed too much pondweed.

"How did you manage to do that?" asked Otley as he towed Willie ashore.

"Do what?" spluttered Willie.

"Fall off a perfectly safe bridge."

"I was looking at my reflection," mumbled Willie, "I . . . er . . . sort of . . . er . . . over balanced."

No one ever fell off the bridge again. Not even Willie. He said once was enough.

And so, once again, the badgers, and Willie, had time to do the things they wanted to do. When they took the raft out it was because they felt like a gentle drift in the dappled shadows and not because someone was in a hurry to get to the other side of the pond.

The problem had been solved and EVERYONE was happy.

WAS IT REAL?

Sometimes, when the sun was shining and there were no chores waiting to be done, Willie would take the raft out to the middle of the pond and let it drift while he lay on his back and dozed. One afternoon he woke from a dream and thought for a moment he was still dreaming.

A large grey bird, with
legs as long as stilts had
flown right over his head.
Willie sat up with a jerk and
rubbed his eyes. He WASN'T
dreaming. It WAS still there.
It was paddling in THEIR pond.
He had never seen such an
important looking bird in the
whole of his life.

He didn't dare shout for Basil and Dewy. The bird was sure to hear him. It might be shy and fly away. Even worse, it might be unfriendly and peck him with its long, sharp beak. Very carefully, and so quietly that he made no noise at all, he rowed to the bank. So far so good. He tiptoed towards the house. The heron, for that was what the bird was, took no notice of him at all. It was standing as still as a statue with painted golden eyes.

'Basil and Dewy are never going to believe this,' thought Willie. He could hardly believe it himself.

Basil and Dewy were indoors making lemonade.

"Th . . . the . . . ther . . . there . . ." Willie was so excited he couldn't get the words out.

Basil was squeezing a lemon. The juice kept squirting into his eyes. He was glad of an excuse to stop squeezing for a moment. He looked at Willie with interest.

"What's the matter?" he asked.

"There . . . there's a bird . . . it's got legs as long . . . as long as THAT." By Willie's measurement the heron had legs as long as broom handles.

Basil grinned. "Yes . . ." he said. "I've got that . . . and what else has it got?"

"It's got a neck as long as . . . THAT." By Willie's measurement the heron had a neck as long as a rolling pin.

"I suppose it's got a beak as long as a toasting fork," said Basil.

"Yes . . . yes it has," said Willie.

Dewy had stopped squeezing now. He was staring at

Willie in amazement.

"Do you think he's been lying in the sun too long?" he asked Basil.

"Either that, or his imagination is working overtime," laughed Basil.

"I tell you there IS!" said Willie stamping his foot. "It's simply enormous . . . it's as big . . . as big as YOU."

"Now we know you're exaggerating," laughed Dewy.

"I'm NOT!" said Willie.

"You are . . ." said Basil. "Stop making up stories and come and squeeze some lemons . . . you'll probably drink most of the lemonade when it's made anyway."

"Shan't!" said Willie, and he stormed out of the house looking like a thunder cloud.

He marched angrily to the pond and faced the heron. He didn't care if it did peck him. "They don't believe you are real," he said. "They think I'm making you up." And just to prove to himself that he wasn't, he dared to touch the heron's spindly leg

The heron turned and gave him a long, haughty stare.

"You ARE real . . . aren't you?" said Willie.

"Of course I am," said the heron. "But are YOU real, you funny creature, that's what I would like to know?"

And without waiting for an answer the heron spread its wings and flew away.

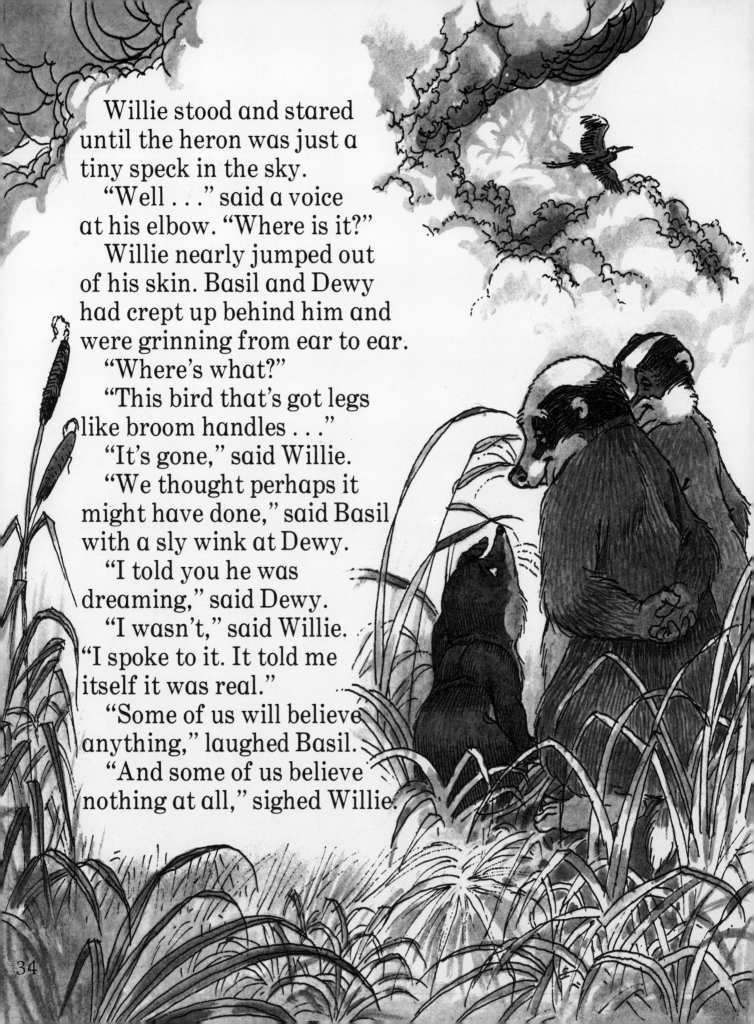

Willie stood and stared
until the heron was just a
tiny speck in the sky.

"Well . . ." said a voice
at his elbow. "Where is it?"

Willie nearly jumped out
of his skin. Basil and Dewy
had crept up behind him and
were grinning from ear to ear.

"Where's what?"

"This bird that's got legs
like broom handles . . ."

"It's gone," said Willie.

"We thought perhaps it
might have done," said Basil
with a sly wink at Dewy.

"I told you he was
dreaming," said Dewy.

"I wasn't," said Willie.
"I spoke to it. It told me
itself it was real."

"Some of us will believe
anything," laughed Basil.

"And some of us believe
nothing at all," sighed Willie.

SOMETHING PRICKLY

In the wood the chestnuts were ripening and falling from the trees. Their prickly cases were everywhere.

"Ouch!" said Basil and hopped about on one foot.

"Why don't you look where you're putting your feet," said Willie and then trod on a spiky nutcase himself.

"OUCH!" he said, twice as loudly as Basil.

"Why don't YOU look where YOU are putting YOUR feet," said Basil and Dewy together.

"I suppose you think that's funny," said Willie.

"It is funny," said Basil, carefully avoiding another of the spiky balls.

"What's inside them anyway?" asked Willie.

"Nuts," said Dewy.

"Don't be rude," said Willie. "I asked a perfectly civil question."

"And I gave you a perfectly civil answer," said Dewy. "Nuts . . ."

Willie glowered and puffed out his chest. He looked as though he might explode.

"I'll show you," said Dewy quickly. He picked up a spiky ball that had a split in its coat and prised it open.

35

He showed Willie the smooth brown nut that had been tucked tightly inside the spiky husk.

"They are very good to eat," he said. He peeled off the brown skin and popped the milky-white nut into his mouth.

"I would like to try one of those," said Willie.

"Then you'd better peel one, hadn't you?" laughed Dewy.
"I suppose you think I can't do it," said Willie and
began to juggle with a ball that seemed to be made from a
million jabbing spikes.
"Ouch! Oh . . . ouch!" he winced.

While Willie juggled and got crosser and crosser but more and more determined not to be beaten, Basil and Dewy gathered a hatful of nuts to take home. At long last, Willie got the nut out of its prickly case. It was very, very tiny and his paws were very, very sore.

"Do you mean to tell me I've gone to ALL that trouble just to get THAT out?" he said crossly. He peeled off the brown skin and put the nut in his mouth. It was gone in one gulp. "They're just not worth the bother," he said.

He was trailing along behind Basil and Dewy, muttering and grumbling to himself when he caught sight of something out of the corner of his eye. He looked quickly at Basil and Dewy. THEY hadn't noticed. He suddenly found something interesting to stop and look at. Then as soon as Basil and Dewy were a safe distance ahead, he scrambled into the leaves and stared with delight at the big, brown prickly ball. It was HUGE. It was GIGANTIC! A prickly something of that size would be worth peeling.

"Ouch . . . oh . . . ouch . . ." he said softly under his breath, as he picked it up and cradled it in his arms. Its prickles were incredibly sharp, but what did that matter? Just think of the size of the nut inside!

He kept his distance behind Dewy and Basil all the way home.

"I'd just like to see their faces when I'm eating this," he said. "But they won't see me because I'll eat it in secret . . ." The prickly ball got heavier and heavier. His tummy began to feel like a pin cushion.

"Where's Willie?" asked Basil when he and Dewy got home.

"He's coming," said Dewy. "I say, he seems to have found something. I wonder what it is?"

"What have you got there?" asked Basil as Willie came round the corner by the shed. Willie was taken completely by surprise. By his reckoning Basil and Dewy should have been safely indoors.

"Where? What? Oh, you mean this," he said, trying to sound casual and unconcerned. He supposed he'd have to share it with them now. "It's a chestnut."

Basil and Dewy stared at him.

"No it isn't," said Dewy.

Willie couldn't argue while he was feeling like a pin cushion, so he put the nut down. And there, right in front of him, it . . . uncurled itself . . . and RAN AWAY.

"Come back!" shouted Willie. "Where do you think you're going?"

"Back to his mother I shouldn't wonder," said Dewy.

"His mother?" Willie didn't understand.

"Don't you know a young hedgehog when you see one?" laughed Basil.

"EEEK!" cried Willie, and all his fur stood on end.
"What WOULD have happened to me if I had tried to peel it?"
He felt quite faint at the thought, but Basil and Dewy
laughed until the tears rolled down their cheeks.

"I don't know why you're laughing," said Willie.
"I don't think it's funny at all."

THE SECRET

Basil had made a bird house and fixed it to a pole in the garden.

"I wish someone would build me a house like that," sighed Willie, as he watched the pigeons move in. He didn't know Basil was standing behind him.

That evening there was a lot of whispering every time Willie left the room. Next morning, as soon as the chores were done, Dewy said, "Get the axe Willie, we're going to do some chopping."

"Do we have to," sighed Willie. He didn't like chopping. It made his back ache. It made him tired.

Basil took him firmly by the shoulder and propelled him outside.

"We need your help," he said. "Now be a good chap and get the axe. We'll be up by the big oak."

Willie knew exactly where the axe was but he spent as much time getting it as he possibly could and then he ambled slower than a snail through the wood.

"You can start there," said Basil, pointing to a thin weedy looking tree. "Chop that down."

"Who? Me?" asked Willie. If he'd known he was going to be the one using the axe he would have taken longer still to find it.

"Yes, you," said Basil. "Dewy and I have got other things to do. When you've chopped that down, you can chop that one . . . and that one . . . and that one . . ." And so that there would be no mistakes, he tied a piece of creeper round each of the four trees. "No slacking, mind . . ."

As soon as Basil and Dewy had gone, Willie put down the axe and sat on a fallen log.

"Cheek . . ." he grumbled. "Leaving me to do the work."

He was still sitting there half an hour later when Dewy and Basil came back with a load of wooden planks.

"Finished already?" asked Basil, though he could see perfectly well Willie hadn't even started.

"Well . . . er . . not exactly . . ." said Willie.

"Well, get on with it then," said Dewy, as he and Basil went off again.

The next time Willie heard them coming back and wasn't caught sitting down. They were carrying the ladder and a piece of rope. They propped the ladder against the trunk of the big oak and Basil climbed up with the rope.

"What are you doing?" asked Willie, leaning on the axe.

"Get on with the chopping," said Dewy.

"I was only asking a simple question . . ." muttered Willie, and he went on mumbling and grumbling to himself all the time he was swinging the axe. "If they're going to be like that I won't bother to ask again," he said to himself.

For some strange reason that Willie couldn't fathom,
Basil and Dewy were hauling pieces of wood into the tree.
   "Stop staring and get on with the chopping," called
Dewy. "Those trunks are part of our plan . . . if you keep us
waiting you'll NEVER know what we're doing, will you?"

When all the trunks were cut, Basil tied the rope
round them and hauled them up into the tree too.
  "You can bring those smaller pieces up now," he called.
  "I seem to be doing twice as much work as anyone else,"
grumbled Willie as he toiled up and down the ladder.

Basil and Dewy made him work in the tree ALL day. Late in the afternoon Basil sent him down to the house to make some sandwiches and a flask of coffee.

"I'm tired," complained Willie. "Can't someone else go?" He couldn't remember the last time he had worked so hard, or for so long, or had such backache. He couldn't understand why Basil and Dewy were looking so cheerful.

"Take your time . . ." called Dewy as Willie plodded off down the footpath.

"Thanks a lot," said Willie. "I suppose that will give YOU time to think of something else for me to do."

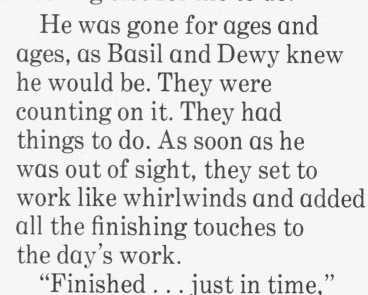

He was gone for ages and ages, as Basil and Dewy knew he would be. They were counting on it. They had things to do. As soon as he was out of sight, they set to work like whirlwinds and added all the finishing touches to the day's work.

"Finished . . . just in time," said Basil as they heard Willie coming back.

What a surprise Willie had.

"It's . . . it's . . . a tree house . . ." he gasped. "We've been building a tree house . . . Why didn't you tell me?"

46

"We wanted it to be a surprise," said Dewy.

"You've been helping us build your own house on a pole," laughed Basil. "We thought as it was going to be your house it was only fair you should do some of the work."

"MY house," gasped Willie. "Is it really MINE?"

"Of course it is," said Basil and Dewy together.

Willie's tiredness, and all his aches and pains, disappeared as though by magic.

"I must be the happiest mole in the world," he sighed, and he looked as though he was too.

47

A . . . A . . . SOMETHING

Dewy was weeding, Willie was pretending to be busy and Basil was on his knees in the cabbage patch.

"Someone has been eating the cabbages," said Basil.

"It wasn't me," said Willie, quickly swallowing a mouthful of peas and dropping the empty pod.

"Look . . ." said Basil. "Holes in all the leaves.
Now who would do a thing like that?"
"EEEK!" cried Willie as Basil looked up. "You've
got a . . . a . . . something . . . on your nose."
"Have I?" said Basil. "What kind of a something?"

"It's moving . . ." cried Willie. "It's moving . . ."

Basil wrinkled his nose and squinted along towards its tip. "It's only a little caterpillar," he said.

"Only! ONLY a caterpillar! Just let a caterpillar try to crawl on ME!" said Willie. "Just let one TRY, that's all, just let one TRY . . . I'd squash it FLAT!"

"Well don't squash this one, or my nose," said Basil and carefully returned the caterpillar to the cabbage leaf from which it had come.

"I don't think you should do that," said Dewy. "It will repay you by making more holes in the cabbages."

"It's got to eat something," said Basil.

"OOOWWW!" It was Willie again.

"What's the matter now?" asked Basil. "Did a caterpillar touch you?"

"There's one walking on me . . . take it off . . . TAKE IT OFF!"

Basil and Dewy looked. They looked carefully, but they could see nothing remotely resembling a caterpillar . . . unless . . .

"You don't mean THIS, do you?" asked Dewy, picking something green, and fat, from Willie's tummy and dangling it in front of his nose.

Willie closed his eyes tightly.

"I don't want to see it . . . take it away."

"Willie . . ." began Dewy sternly.

"I won't look . . . I WON'T!" said Willie defiantly.

"If you do you will see what . . ."

"I won't . . . I won't . . . I don't want a thing like THAT

getting near MY nose."

"Open your eyes!"
ordered Basil.

"Shan't! Won't! Can't!
Not going to!"

"If you don't I'll put it
back," threatened Dewy.

"You wouldn't dare!"
said Willie, but just to make
sure he quickly opened one eye
and peeped. He closed it
again, just as quickly, when
he saw Dewy was still dangling
the fat . . . green . . . horrible . . .
THING . . . in front of his nose.

"We're wasting our time,"
said Dewy. "I'm going indoors
to get supper. I'm taking
THIS with me. Willie will
have to come indoors too if he
wants to see what it is."

"I don't WANT to see it,"
said Willie and he stood right
where he was, with his eyes
tightly closed until he was
sure Dewy and Basil and the
THING had gone.

When it felt safe he opened his eyes and carefully stepped out of the cabbage patch. He was going as far away from cabbage eating caterpillars as he could. How was he to know cabbages weren't the only thing caterpillars lived on. But what Willie didn't see, Willie didn't worry about.

He sat beside the pond until he felt hungry and then he went to the back door. He knocked loudly.

"YOU don't have to knock," said Basil when he saw who it was. "YOU live here. YOU can come straight in."

"Not with THAT thing in the house," said Willie.

Dewy appeared beside Basil and held up a jar.

"It's in here," he said.

"Keep it away from me," said Willie, with a shudder.

"It won't hurt you," said Dewy, staring at Willie's head and trying not to giggle. "Here . . . read the label."

Very, very cautiously, Willie leant towards the jar.

"Go on . . . read what it says," urged Basil.

"Dangerous . . ." read Willie with a sharp intake of breath. "Found crawling on Willie. An empty pea pod."

There was a long, long silence as Willie looked at the empty pea pod, and Dewy and Basil looked at the striped caterpillar looping the loop over Willie's head.

"Well, it looked like a giant caterpillar," said Willie at last. "How was I to know it wasn't?"

"All you had to do was open your eyes," said Dewy.

"You should have told me what it was," said Willie.

"We don't have to tell you everything," laughed Dewy, as Basil slipped behind Willie and secretly removed the real caterpillar and put it on a leafy plant. That was something else they wouldn't tell Willie about. He would have made far too much fuss.

A NIGHT OUT

Something had jumped across the path and under a leaf, right in front of Basil and Willie. Something tiny.

"It's a jumping stone!" shrieked Willie.

"Don't be silly, stones don't jump," said Basil. He lifted the leaf to see what it was that was trying to hide.

"OWWW . . .!" shrieked Willie as the tiny thing jumped again.

"Stop doing that . . . you'll frighten it," said Basil.

"It's frightening ME," said Willie. "But I suppose that doesn't matter."

"It's a baby frog," said Basil. "Look!" He had picked up the tiny thing. "Take a peep, it won't hurt you."

Willie dared to look . . . and the tiny frog jumped again.

"OW!" shrieked Willie, jumping half a yard into the air. "It punched me on the nose."

"Sometimes . . ." sighed Basil, ". . . you are SO silly."

"Spiteful thing," said Willie. "Jumping about like that and throwing punches when a mole least expects it . . . it shouldn't be allowed."

"Look! There's another," said Dewy. "And another." There were little frogs everywhere.

Everywhere Willie stepped a frog jumped out at him.
And every time a frog jumped, Willie jumped as well.
"Where have they all come from?" he wailed.
"From the pond of course," laughed Basil. "The
tadpoles have grown their legs."

"There are millions of tadpoles in the pond," gasped Willie. "Do you mean to tell me they're ALL going to turn into frogs?"

"Probably," said Basil. Without saying a word Willie dived through the shed door and banged it shut behind him.

"What are you doing in there?" called Basil through the window.

"I'm staying here till all those frogs have hopped away," said Willie.

"I do believe he's afraid of them," said Dewy.

"I'm NOT!" said Willie. But he was still in the shed at bedtime.

"Have they all gone?" he called through a crack in the door.

"How can we tell?" said Basil. "It's dark out here."

"They're probably asleep," said Dewy. "Be brave Willie, make a run for it . . ."

"I might," said Willie. "Then again I might not . . . they might all be waiting out there to pounce on me . . . no . . . I've decided . . . you can bring my bed out here . . . I'll be much safer here . . ."

"You'll have to make do with the camp bed," said Basil. "If you want to sleep in your proper bed you can jolly well come indoors."

"I don't know why YOU'RE grumbling," grumbled Willie. "I'm the one who is under attack." He opened the shed door just wide enough for them to push the camp bed through the gap, then shut it again quickly. He didn't sleep very well. In fact he hardly slept a wink. The walls of the shed kept creaking. Once he thought he heard something squeak. He could hear someone breathing but he thought that was himself.

"Perhaps I should have gone indoors," he sighed, as the first light of morning shone through a knot hole.

"Why? Don't you like it here?" asked a deep, gravelly voice, from somewhere under the camp bed. "I ALWAYS sleep here . . . I find it very comfortable."

Willie's shriek almost blew the roof off the shed. He almost pushed the door off its hinges in his hurry to get out. He ran across the garden and banged at the back door shouting, "Let me in . . . LET ME IN . . ."

It took a hot drink and a piece of Dewy's chocolate cake to calm him down.

"There . . . there's someone in the shed . . ." he said. "They . . . they've been there ALL night . . . with MEEEE!"

Basil and Dewy went at once to investigate. When they saw who the intruder was they invited him to the house.

"Meet Grandpa Frog," said Basil with an enormous grin.
"Pleased to meet you, again," said the frog.
Willie recognised the voice and fainted clean away. He
had run away from the tiny baby frogs and spent the whole
night with an ENORMOUS GIANT of a frog under his bed!